My BIG Boy Bed

written by
Eve Bunting

illustrated by
Maggie Smith

✳

Clarion Books
New York

Clarion Books
a Houghton Mifflin Company imprint
215 Park Avenue South, New York, NY 10003
Text copyright © 2003 by Eve Bunting
Illustrations copyright © 2003 by Maggie Smith

The illustrations were executed in watercolor.
The text was set in 20-point Gill Sans Bold Condensed.

Printed in Singapore

Library of Congress Cataloging-in-Publication Data

Bunting, Eve
My big boy bed / by Eve Bunting ; pictures by Maggie Smith.
p. cm.
Summary: A little boy celebrates all the things he can do now that he has a big boy bed.
ISBN: 0-618-17742-6 (alk. paper)
[1. Beds—Fiction. 2. Growth—Fiction.] I. Smith, Maggie, ill. II. Title.
PZ7.B91527 My 2003
[E]—dc21   2002013366

TWP   10 9 8 7 6 5 4 3 2 1

For Shane, with love
—E. B.

For Joann H.—Making books is always fun with you!
—M. S.

Goodbye, crib.
Now I've got my big boy bed.

Mom and I bought big boy sheets,
and a big boy quilt,

and *The Little Fat Book of Fire Trucks.*

7

While Mom spread out the quilt,
I showed *The Little Fat Book of Fire Trucks* to
Whiskers. "Big boys can read in bed," I told him.

I can bounce high, high on my big boy bed.

I can go under it,
and be a dog,
and scare Whiskers.

"Grrr,

grrr."

13

There is more room now for Teddy to sleep with me.
There's room for my painted clay lizard,
and Hippo,
and *The Little Fat Book of Fire Trucks.*

And my blankie.

Whiskers can sleep with us, too.

Mom and Dad tuck me into my big boy bed.
But I can get out again
anytime I want.

Except that they call:
"Donny! Get back in bed this minute."

21

How do they know? That's what I want to know.

But sometimes I get out again anyway.
I tiptoe across the room . . .

. . . and look into the crib at my new little brother, who's snuggling there.

I poke my fingers through the bars
and touch his hand
and whisper,
"Good night, little baby!"

Then I climb back in my big boy bed,
and go to sleep . . .

. . . while the moon shines through my window
and my clown lamp smiles at me,

all through the night.